This book
belongs to:

....

Published in Great Britain by Brimax,
An imprint of Autumn Publishing Group

Published in the US in 2004 by Byeway Books Inc,
Lenexa KS 66219 Tel 866.4BYEWAY

www.byewaybooks.com

Printed in China

Charlie Chick's new nest

BRIMAX

Charlie Chick shares his nest with his six brothers and sisters. Sharing a nest can be warm and snug, but it can sometimes be crowded, too!

"Oh, I wish you would all stop wriggling and moving around!" sighed Charlie, as one of the other chicks turned and squashed him into a corner!

As if that wasn't enough, another chick was sitting on poor Charlie's tail!

"This is so uncomfortable!" squawked Charlie. "There's no room in here!"

At last, after moving very slowly and carefully, Charlie managed to find a space to lie down.

"Ah, that's better," sighed Charlie.

But as soon as Charlie closed his eyes to take a nap, another chick's fluffy wing tap-tap-tapped him on the head!

"I love you all very much but I wish there was more room in this nest," Charlie told his fidgety brothers and sisters. "Wouldn't it be wonderful if we could stretch our wings whenever we liked?"

But the other chicks were too busy trying to make room for themselves to listen to Charlie.

"I said..." began Charlie. But before he finished what he was saying, the tiny chick found himself tumbling out of the nest!

Luckily, Charlie landed on soft ground. Rubbing his bottom, Charlie looked up at the nest. His brothers and sisters hadn't even noticed that he had fallen out!

Well, I guess I won't be missed, thought Charlie!

Now that Charlie had found himself on the ground, he decided it was time to look for a new nest.

There must be a comfortable home for me somewhere, thought Charlie, as he wandered around the farmyard.

Charlie cheered up when he found a hat. It was covered in dirt and cobwebs.

"This hat looks a little old and worn but I'm sure I can make it into a perfect home," decided Charlie, happily.

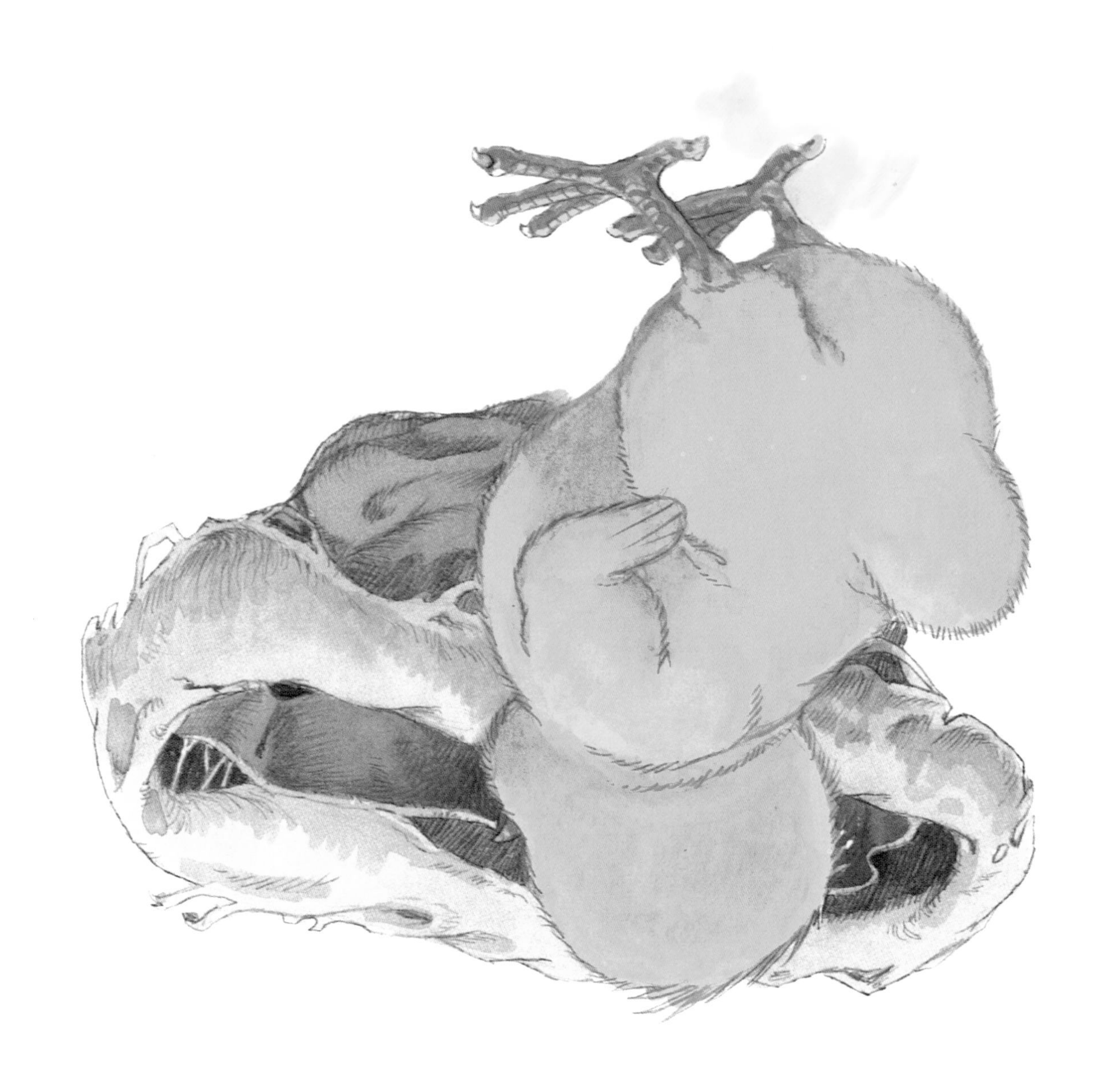

Jumping up on to the brim of the old hat, Charlie peered inside. "Just as I thought. There will be plenty of room for me to grow and spread my wings in here!" Charlie said to himself.

But before he could move into his new home, Charlie had lots of work to do. First he had to jump up and down on the hat to loosen the dirt and shake away the cobwebs.

"Wheee! This is fun!" chirped Charlie, as he sprang up into the air. "In fact, it's almost like flying!"

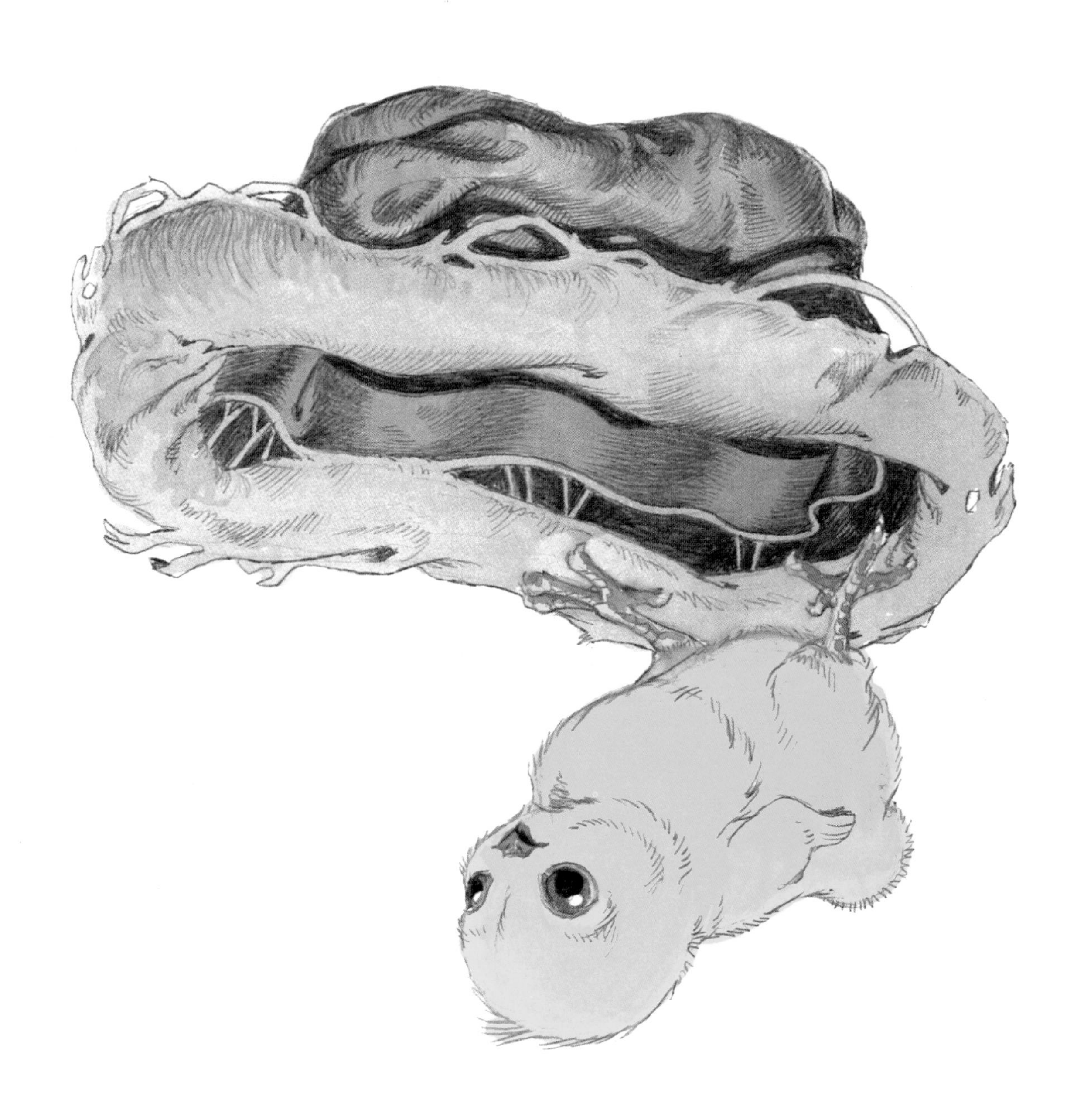

When the hat was clean and tidy, Charlie went off to search for some soft, warm things to line his new home.

This is perfect, thought Charlie, finding a silky bird's feather lying on the ground. Picking up the feather with his beak, Charlie carried it all the way back to his nest.

"Dear me! I'm going to have to work faster if I want to move into my home today," Charlie said.

Building a new home was so exciting!

Next, Charlie set off in the opposite direction. He found some soft, fluffy dandelions growing in the farmer's field. "I'm sure the farmer won't mind if I pick a few of these dandelions," chirped Charlie.

One by one, Charlie carried the dandelions back to the hat.

"These will make my nest so soft and comfortable to sleep in," smiled Charlie.

As he walked along, some of the dandelion seeds blew into the air and tickled Charlie's beak.

At last the hat was ready. Standing on the brim of the hat, Charlie admired his new nest. The silky feather and the soft, fluffy dandelions made a lining that would last for a long, long time.

It was quite hard work for a little chick, but now he had a warm, soft nest of his own. Charlie felt rather proud of himself and there was plenty of room for him to sleep.

There was just one more thing left to do...

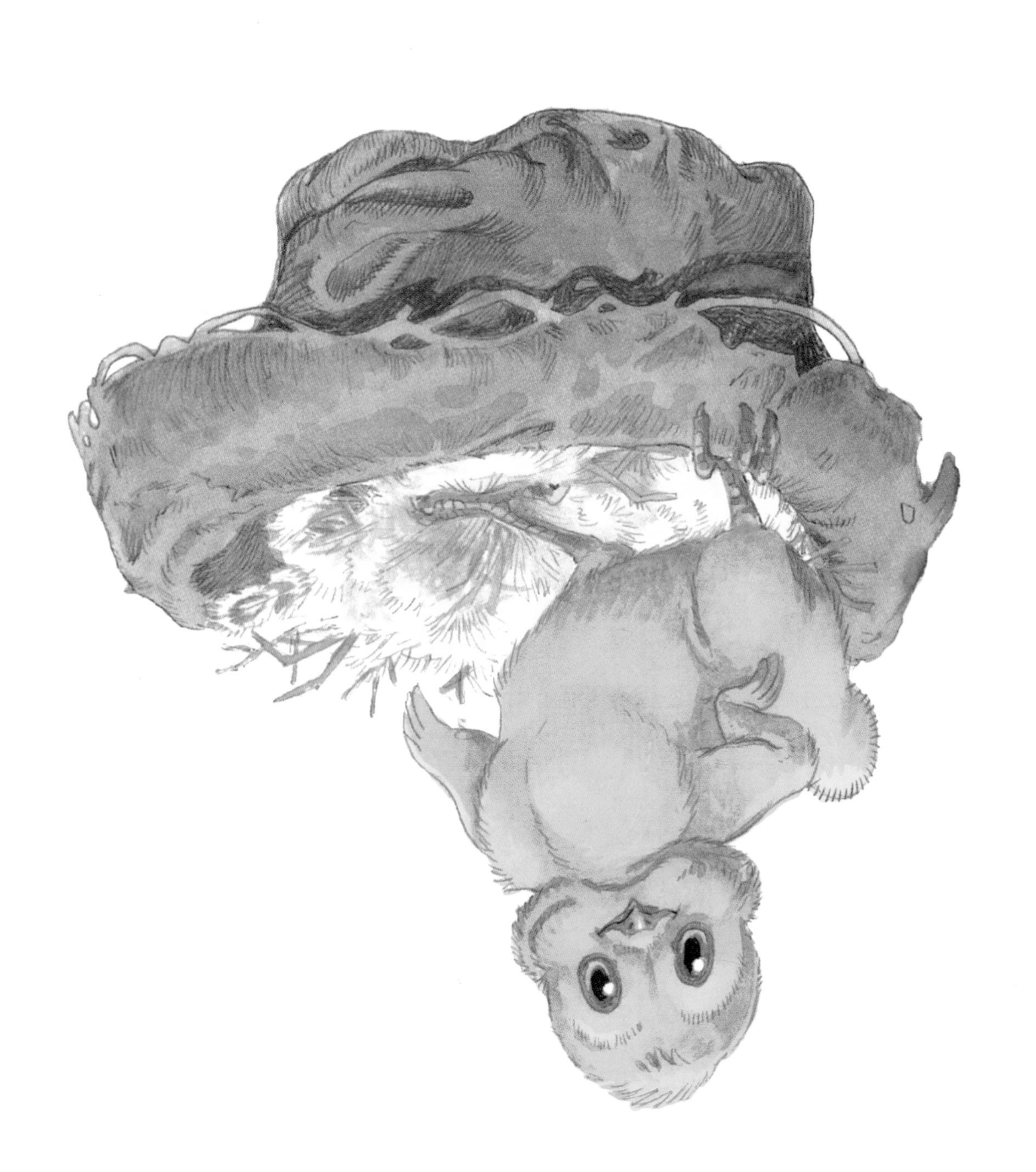

Charlie hopped on to the soft, fluffy lining inside the hat. Then he wriggled and jiggled around until he was comfortable.

"It's so nice not to have to worry about being pushed out of my nest," yawned Charlie, as he closed his weary eyes.

Stretching his legs, Charlie was soon snug and warm and fast asleep!

Goodnight, Charlie. Sweet dreams.

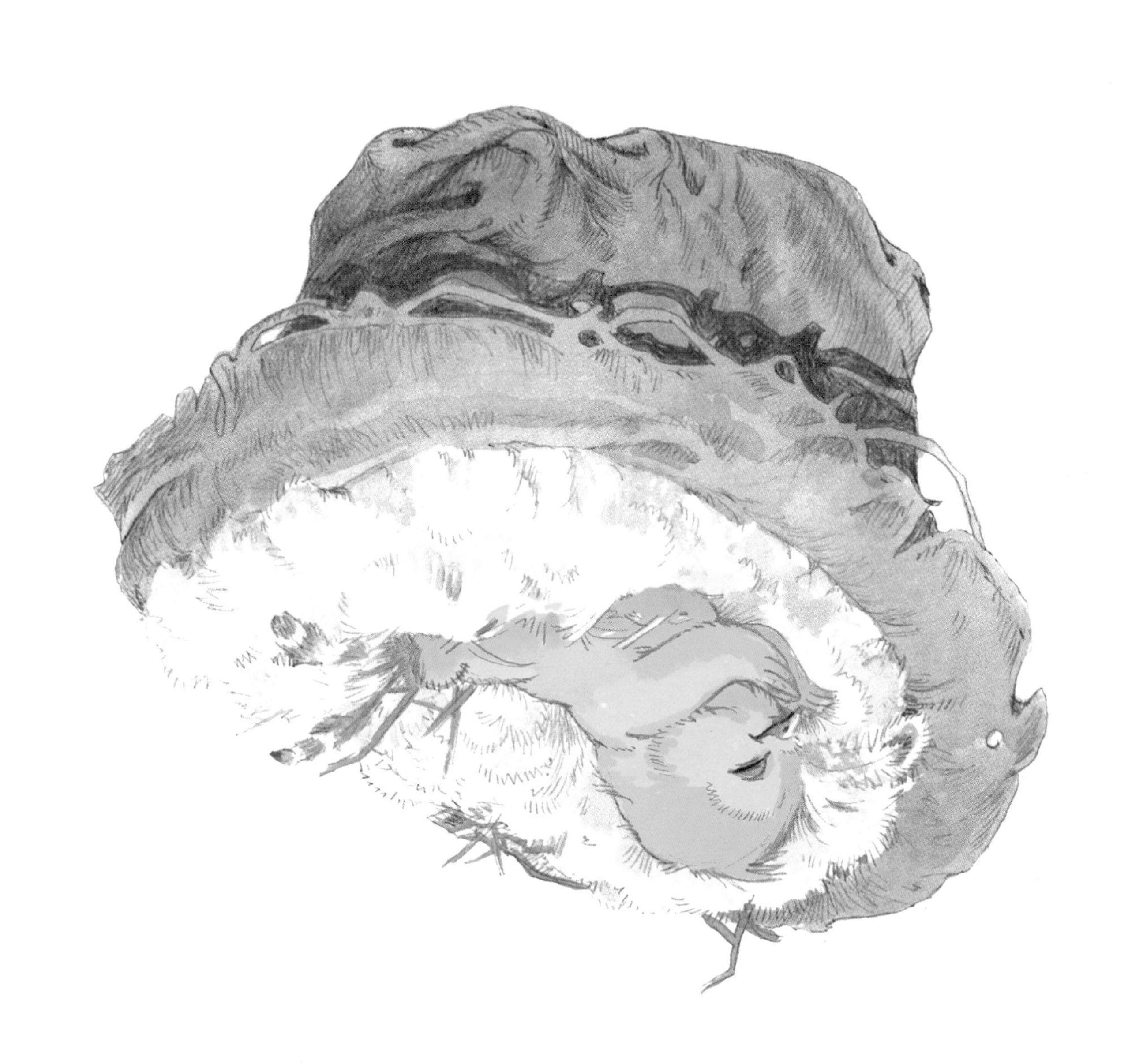

Do you know?

1 How many brothers and sisters does Charlie have?

2 Where did another chick tap Charlie?

3 What did Charlie tumble out of?

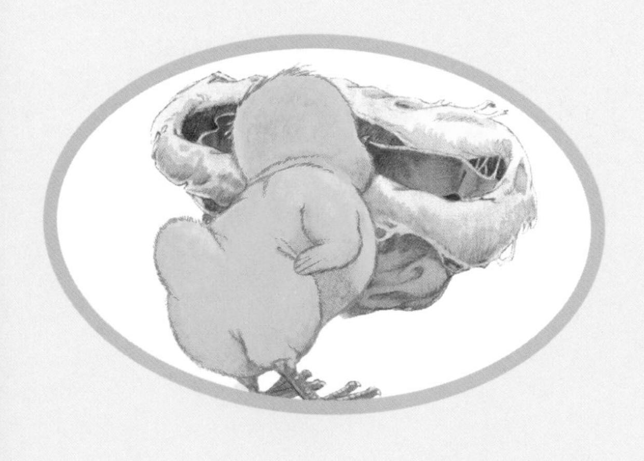

4 What did Charlie use to make himself a new nest?

5 What tickled Charlie's beak?

6 How many feathers did Charlie use to line his nest?

Answers:

1. Six. 2. On his head. 3. A nest. 4. An old hat. 5. A dandelion. 6. One.